Devotion

Prayers to the Gods of the Greeks

Devotion
Prayers to the Gods of the Greeks

by
Hearthstone

Printed by Lulu in the United States of America
http://www.lulu.com/

Cover image taken from a Dionysos mask in the author's collection.

To Aphrodite
and
to Dionysos.

Contents

About This Book

A number of years ago I found myself called by the Greek gods—specifically, by Aphrodite. I had been pagan for years, but this was something new. I became, immediately, a hard polytheist—someone who perceives the gods as individuals, rather than as aspects of a greater godhead. I became acquainted with the community of Hellenic reconstructionists, people who strive to revive the religion of the ancient Greeks and adapt it to today's world, and the work they have been doing, and adopted a semi-reconstructionist religious practice; these prayers were written from that point of view, but I hope not limited by it. We all have to find our own way to the gods. I hope what I've written will be useful for those who are travelling many different roads.

The Gods

We all know the Greek gods. They are a part of our world, of our culture. We grow up seeing references to them in literature, poetry and art. We see them in movies, on television. We *know* them. We know that Athena loves wisdom and is the patroness of clever heroes; we know that Demeter brings life to the land, and mourns Her daughter each year when the earth grows barren. We know of Apollo's many tragic loves, and of Dionysos' devotion to His Ariadne. We read these stories as children, and although they may have been presented as the foolishness of the ancients, mythological truth is always seen for what it is, and we *know* the gods.

However, while some books on mythology and ancient Greek religion treat the deities as a sort of godly Justice League, saying that Aphrodite is the goddess of love, Ares the god of war, Poseidon the god of the sea, and so forth, this is a very simplistic way to look at them. The gods may each have particular areas of interest, but that doesn't mean that these areas define the deities. It is less a matter of action than of character, and the character of a god is far too complex to be so easily categorized.

In my experience, the gods of the Greeks come as a set—-as a family—and even though we may not be as close to some as to others, they are connected to each other, and to those of us who worship or honor any one of them. It's a good thing, when one is devoted to even one of the Greek gods, to pay one's respects to the rest of the "family" in some way.

The Prayers

A while ago I came across a collection of modern prayers to the Greek gods. I was surprised to see that no prayers to Aphrodite were included; this, to a devotee of the goddess, was unacceptable, and to my surprise I found myself writing one. That was the beginning of this collection, which is now complete. I began writing because I saw a need for it. Certainly many other people have written, and are writing, beautiful prayers to the gods, but at that time these were not as easy to find.

And there were other reasons to write, beyond necessity. I have found writing for the gods to be one of the best ways to deepen my understanding of them, and to develop my relationship with them. It's not so easy, these days, to build temples or to erect statues. However, it's well within the ability of any of us to write a prayer, and to pour out a libation of wine or leave an offering of food or flowers. In a way, putting these prayers into a book and making them available is itself an offering. Many of these prayers have been available online for some time, and will remain so, because I think it's important that words of praise to the gods be seen and shared, but there is something about having the words on paper, something solid that I can hold in my hands, that led me to put this book together.

I hope that the prayers in this book please the reader, but I hope more that you will find them useful. I'm no poet. Function, not form, was foremost in my mind while I wrote, and I tried to say something important about each god as I wrote for Him or Her. If anyone is able to gain a better understanding of the gods by reading or using this book, it has served its purpose.

Hestia

Hestia

Hestia, tender of the hearth,
first among the gods,
you sit at the center;
steadily burns your flame.
Your warmth draws us,
your gentle light guides us, leading
us sure-footed through cold and dark
to our own place,
where your presence welcomes us
and eases our hearts.
Without your touch our homes grow chill,
our hearts empty.
Wherever family and friends are joined,
you are there.
Wherever we are safe and content,
you are there.
Wherever we are most comforted,
you are there.
Wherever we find we most belong,
you are there.
Revered Hestia,
first and most necessary one,
gracious goddess,
I praise you and ask your blessing.

Hestia

Hestia, ancient one,
guardian of the hearth,
bringer of light and warmth,
dweller in flame.
A candle seen
in a distant window,
deep red-gold embers
buried in soft ash,
a welcoming fire
in winter's stark cold,
in all these we feel your touch,
dear Hestia.
Most honored goddess,
to whom we offer
always first and last.
Wise one, peaceful one,
you who lives
at the center of each home,
we thank you for comfort
and family,
for belonging
and security.
Revered Hestia,
we praise and honor you.

Hestia

Gentle Hestia, sitting at the fire,
 at the heart
of each home, goddess revered
 above all others.
Bringer of quiet comfort,
 of belonging,
of peace, of a place
 of love and family,
of the strength to hold together
 against all ill,
provider of serenity,
 I honor you.
Hestia, seen in candleglow
 and soft shadow,
I pray to you. Help me
 to see you in my work,
to make our home a refuge
 from care and distress.
Give me competence, efficiency,
 wisdom;
give me quick sharp eyes
 to see what must be done,
give me will to do it.
 Goddess, bless my home.

Zeus

Zeus

Zeus, mightiest of those
 who walk Olympos' halls,
none can long deny your will,
 you who rules the gods
themselves. You send the storms,
 the sharp claps of thunder,
the bright bolts of lightning
 that strike at your command.
Great Zeus, who we call on
 as defender, who we
pray to for victory,
 whose honors are the highest;
Zeus of many festivals;
 Zeus of many names;
kindly Zeus, Zeus the provider,
 guardian of guests,
protector of children;
 Zeus the all-powerful,
mate to stately Hera,
 father of gods and men;
Zeus by whom oaths are sworn;
 Zeus the wise and the just;
Father Zeus, I honor you
 and ask your blessing.

Zeus

Zeus, greatest
among Olympos' mighty,
father of many, gods and men,
you are.
In the soft distant rumble
of thunder,
clouds growing heavy,
deep darkening skies,
torrents of rain,
flashes of bright lightning,
in these we see your hand,
most honored one.
Father Zeus, storm-bringer,
kind provider,
all-powerful ruler
of the heavens,
guardian of children
and travellers,
we thank you for rain
upon fruit and field,
for protection
and for victory.
O peerless Zeus,
we praise and honor you.

Zeus

Father Zeus, holder of lightning,
    master of storms,
ruler of fair Olympos
    and all who there dwell.
All is within your power,
    all bow to your will,
great Zeus who hears all oaths,
    who sees justice done,
who watches over all
    with benevolent gaze,
whose blessings are great;
    awesome Zeus, I honor you.
Guardian of our homes,
    protector of our children,
kind Zeus, I pray to you.
    Guide me to be just,
to act with honor,
    to keep my promises,
to welcome guests freely,
    to do what is right.
Watch over our home
    and bring to it abundance,
O Zeus; watch over our children,
    shield them from harm.

Hera

Hera

I praise you, great Hera,
        fair bride of mighty Zeus,
mother of stout Ares
        and skillful Hephaistos,
beautiful queen who walks
        Olympos' golden halls.
Magnificent temples are yours,
        glorious goddess;
with libations and festivals
        are you honored,
Hera, with your fathomless eyes,
        your even gaze,
your measured step, your poise
        and grace beyond compare.
To each wedding day you bring joy,
        most honored one;
by your will do lovers join
        in lawful marriage,
as partners form a household,
        begin a family.
Brilliant and strong-willed
        defender of marriage,
great Hera, I honor you
        and ask your blessing.

Hera

Noble Hera,
        fair bride of gloried Zeus,
awesome goddess
        of might unparalleled.
In wedding vows
        entered into with joy,
in well-tossed covers
        on a marriage bed,
in husbands and wives
        together 'til death,
in these things you take joy,
        gracious goddess.
Hera, all-seeing
        friend of the faithful,
staunch defender
        of home and family,
great goddess
        of power unknowable,
we thank you
        for your blessings on partners
and children,
        on kin and on lineage.
Renowned Hera,
        we praise and honor you.

Hera

Stately Hera, glorious queen
    of fair Olympos,
comely you are,
    your shining beauty unsurpassed.
Great daughter of Kronos,
    defender of cities,
deep-eyed goddess,
    chosen bride of thundering Zeus,
mighty guardian
    of the marriage oath and bond,
graceful one, vital one,
    I praise and honor you.
Sublime Hera, swift of thought,
    certain of action
I pray to you. Grant me
    strength of will, O goddess,
help me to know my worth,
    to act with confidence
and passion, to risk wisely,
    to freely speak my mind.
Bless my marriage bed,
    my vows, my devotion.
Peerless Hera, watchful one,
    I ask your favor.

Poseidon

Splendid Poseidon,
        husband of fair Amphitrite,
father to the lovely nymphs
        of river and sea,
all waters comprise your realm.
        O most honored one,
a force so powerful are you,
        none can withstand
your might. At your will seas rise,
        ships are torn apart,
and sailors are given
        both life and livelihood.
And yet have you given
        great gifts to mankind:
the horse, that most noble beast,
        is your creation;
the fish in your seas feed many,
        O Poseidon;
and springs of pure water
        do appear at your touch.
Mighty Poseidon,
        you who rules the deep ocean
and all its creatures,
        I praise and honor you.

Poseidon,
        raging lord of the deep,
master of sea-storm,
        ocean-dwelling god.
Thundering hoofbeats
        across grassy plains,
white-capped waves,
        burnished stones along the shore,
taste of salt spray,
        sapphire-blue horizon,
in these we know you,
        great Poseidon.
Poseidon,
        holder of the sea's treasures,
friend of adventurer
        and merchant,
your hands gently guiding ships
        to harbor,
we thank you for safe journeys,
        mighty one,
for swift travel
        beyond our own borders.
Poseidon,
        we praise and honor you.

Poseidon, dark-haired god
of all waters,
by whose will alone
do sailors fare in safety.
Lord of the black sea depths,
swirling dark and deep,
swift in thought, sure in deed,
fervent in feeling,
the ocean's caprice is yours,
O Poseidon;
overwhelming one,
I praise and honor you.
Mighty Poseidon,
unfathomable one,
I pray to you. You at whose touch
sweet water springs forth,
at whose whim the earth breaks open
beneath our feet,
whose pure power we feel in our bones
and our blood,
show me life's essence, life's rage;
pull me like the tide;
grant me safe harbor at last,
shield me from storms.

Demeter

Demeter

Honored Demeter,
        mother of Persephone,
I praise you.
        Fair-haired bringer of bounty,
all growing things, sweet fruits
        and golden grains, are yours;
willingly you provide us
        what is most needful.
Kind though you are,
        when each year the harvest is done,
then, noble Demeter,
        is your power revealed.
As you mourn
        your beloved daughter's departure,
the earth mourns with you,
        and all see what would soon be,
what would become of all life,
        great one, without you.
Without you
        would the fruitful land be barren.
Without your gifts
        would its people starve and perish.
O Demeter, mighty goddess,
        I honor you.

Demeter

Demeter,
praiseworthy goddess of grain,
beloved mother
of Persephone.
In golden-brown fields
flowing in the wind,
trees heavy with fruit,
the thanksgiving feast,
tender devotion
of mother and child,
in these we find you,
most revered goddess.
Demeter,
giver of life's greatest needs,
whose joy and sorrow are felt
by the earth
and by all of us
who dwell upon her,
we thank you
for your unending bounty,
for spring's green leaves
and autumn's rich harvest.
Great Demeter,
we praise and honor you.

Demeter

Honored Demeter,
    rooted in the dark earth,
tender shoots and golden sheaves alike
    are yours.
Noble goddess,
    fair-haired provider of reward
to those who work the land,
    trading sweat and toil
for fruit and grain;
    mother of Persephone,
your will and devotion turn the world,
    the seasons.
Demeter, awe-inspiring goddess,
    wrathful one,
endless one, I pray to you.
    Grant me hope in despair,
love and loyalty
    so fierce no foe can best me,
sufficiency, growth, transformation.
    Demeter,
bring me through darkness,
    temper my spirit,
show me the joy within pain,
    the life within cold soil.

Hades

Mighty Hades, dweller in the depths,
I honor you.
The world was divided,
one brother took the sky,
another the sea,
and to you was given
the underworld, where all
who live will someday rest.
Kindly one, you welcome
the dead at journey's end
as in your land
they resume a life after life.
Golden-haired Persephone
you chose for your bride,
to be your wife and your queen,
and to share your throne.
As you rule under the earth,
yours are its riches.
All the wealth of the earth is yours,
O great Hades,
bright gold and precious gems,
all are within your realm.
Hades, O revered one,
I praise and honor you.

Hades

Mighty Hades, great lord
        of wealth and souls,
who dwells in the solemn depths
        of the earth.
In the subtle scent
        of funeral flowers,
in thin white gravestones
        with weathered markings,
in bittersweet thoughts
        of loved ones gone,
in these we feel your strength,
        honored Hades.
Hades, kind one
        who welcomes the dead,
holder of all precious metals
        and stones,
noble bridegroom
        of fair Persephone
we thank you for guarding those
        who have passed,
for comfort in pain,
        for memories dear.
Hades, great one,
        we praise and honor you.

Hades

Hades, lord of the underworld,
        host of the dead,
stern holder of the boundary
        between death and life.
Cold flesh becomes spirit,
        bright eyes glint from shadows,
lovers long parted unite,
        families join once more—
kind one, fearsome one,
        all this you see and welcome,
all this you encompass,
        light in dark, love in death.
Hades unseen, lord of all
        who have lived and died,
I pray to you. Master of dreams,
        giver of wealth,
receiver of those most dear to us,
        lost to us,
treasures all, all within your realm.
        Great Hades,
guardian of all
        who have passed to your kingdom,
gracious god to whom we all will go,
        I praise you.

Athena

Athena

I praise you, great Athena,
        child of Zeus alone,
all in armor born,
        fair maid and fearsome warrior.
Defender of cities
        and patron of heroes,
swiftly will victory come
        to those you favor.
Revered daughter of wisdom,
        clear thought you provide,
and foresight and cunning
        do mark those you have touched.
All skilled crafts are yours as well,
        weaving and spinning
and clever stitchery;
        you gift us, Athena,
with a keen eye, steady hand,
        and nimble fingers.
Grey-eyed Athena,
        mighty one, friend to mankind
and provider of gifts
        both wonderful and useful,
O glorious goddess,
        I praise and honor you.

Shining Athena,
        swift aegis-bearer,
friend of warriors,
        fair daughter of Zeus.
In bravery,
        in find hand stitchery,
in knowledge
        and in understanding,
in crisp, clean thought,
        in artistry and skill,
in these, your realms,
        we see your dextrous hand.
Glorious Athena,
        wisest of gods,
guardian of bold-hearted
        adventurers,
guide of craftsmen,
        defender of cities,
we thank you for clear minds
        and steady hearts,
for just victories
        and keen-edged swords.
Peerless Athena,
        we praise and honor you.

Athena

Athena, flint-eyed daughter
        of excellent Zeus,
clear-headed goddess,
        bold-hearted patron of craft.
Bright Athena, passion guided
        by forethought,
kind one who draws near us,
        who flees no battle,
your favor sought by many,
        your presence so strong,
so penetrating,
        so unmistakable.
Athena, shining war-maid,
        child of wisdom,
I pray to you. Precision
        and unmuddled thought
I ask of you, crisp reason
        and blessed clarity,
surety and conviction,
        quick wit and quick action.
Give me eyes to see far,
        to see true, to see within;
give me heart to bear it,
        give me strength to hold fast.

Apollo

I praise you, Apollo,
brother of Artemis,
noble son of Leto
and thundering Zeus.
Through you have prophecies been made
and come to pass;
far-famed were your priestesses
at sacred Delphi,
and still you provide seers
divine inspiration.
Far-shooter, shining one,
sender of plagues you are
and yet great healing as well
is in your power.
Youth is ever yours,
most excellent Apollo,
you who so loves beauty
and logic and learning;
music is dear to you,
who plays upon the lyre
with sound so sweet
no other's playing can compare.
O brilliant Apollo,
I praise and honor you.

Brilliant Apollo,
giver of far-sight,
swift are your arrows,
sure is your aim.
In intellect, quick
and rational thought,
in science and medicine,
healing and health,
and always in beauty,
music and art,
in these we see you,
great son of Zeus.
Matchless Apollo,
archer without flaw,
dream-granting friend
of seeker and seer,
patron of scholar
and philosopher,
we thank you for reason,
for art's keen eye,
for health for those ailing
in body or soul.
Bright Apollo,
we praise and honor you.

Apollo, radiant son
        of thundering Zeus,
far-seeing, far-shooting,
        distant yet observing.
Shining Apollo, your arrows
        pierce any shield,
your keen eye finds each target
        with unerring aim.
Apollo, wise one, your oracles
        force clear thought
upon the desperate;
        I praise and honor you.
Bright Apollo, patron
        of beauty and reason,
I pray to you. Grant me balance,
        grant me insight,
grant me inspiration.
        Father of Asklepios,
keep all ill health from my home,
        from my family.
Foreknowledge grant me as needed,
        and with it eyes
to see true, undeceived
        by hope, by desire.

Artemis

Artemis

Artemis I praise,
    sister of bright Apollo,
first-born of blessed Leto,
    dear child of Zeus.
Fairest among maidens,
    you roam the wilderness;
the enchanting nymphs
    are your friends and companions.
You take joy in wood and meadow,
    swift-footed one,
you who loves dance and games,
    you who wins every race.
As the wild lands are yours,
    so too are the wild beasts;
huntress you are—with bow your skill
    is unsurpassed,
always do your arrows
    find their mark. Artemis,
O kindly one, you ease
    the sharp pains of childbirth,
and you are the fiercest protector
    of children.
O luminous goddess,
    I praise and honor you.

Artemis

Luminous Artemis,
daughter of Leto,
unsurpassed goddess,
guardian of children.
In all wild things
—wild lands, wild beasts—
in clear-eyed precision,
in flawless aim,
in freedom and motion,
in athlete's grace,
in all these we know you,
radiant one.
Shining Artemis,
huntress unequaled,
beloved companion
of nymphs and maidens,
swift-footed wanderer
in wood and field,
we thank you
for skill and agility,
for heart-pounding effort,
for love of the chase.
Fair Artemis,
we praise and honor you.

Artemis

Artemis, light-footed maiden,
 child of great Zeus
and blessed Leto, sharp-eyed one
 whose aim never fails.
Luminous Artemis,
 sure-stepping huntress,
graceful one who takes joy
 in dance and in contests,
ruthless protector of children
 and young women,
kind one to whom mothers turn
 in their travail.
Artemis, deer-slayer,
 guardian of untamed life,
I pray to you.
 Dark-eyed mistress of animals,
in thick-grown woods
 and sun-soaked fields we know you,
in the maddening chase,
 in the fire in our lungs,
in skill and precision,
 in the body's memory;
grant me understanding
 of such chaste passion.

Hermes

Hermes

I praise you, bright Hermes,
        clever son of great Zeus.
On the day you were born
        was your craftiness known,
you whose cattle-theft angered
        brother Apollo,
whose quick words appeased him,
        whose lyre-gift made him friend.
Bringer of luck, good fortune
        ever follows you,
who is so dear to merchant
        and gambler alike.
Friend of travellers,
        you watch us on our journeys,
honored Hermes, and see us
        safely home once more,
fleet-footed one whose agile wit
        may accomplish
what strength and wisdom cannot.
        God of the crossroads,
guide of the dead,
        messenger of the blessed gods,
Hermes so swift and sure,
        I praise and honor you.

Swift Hermes,
provider of fair fortune,
who travels freely
among the worlds.
In pennies found,
in laughter and delight,
in messages trifling
and essential,
in unexpected twists
of our life's plan,
with these you touch us,
genial son of Zeus.
O Hermes, guide of souls,
light-hearted one,
swift as thought; you know
the depth of impulse,
quick-witted god
of those who live by luck.
We thank you for the path unworn,
for cleverness,
for gifts unearned,
for change unbidden.
Excellent Hermes,
we praise and honor you.

Hermes

Quick-witted Hermes,
        welcome in all the worlds,
fleet-footed son of Zeus,
        clever cattle-thief.
Hermes, kind-hearted one,
        unpredictable one,
impetuous, scheming,
        fortunate, wise,
shimmering rippling surface
        above dark depths,
Hermes, familiar one,
        I praise and honor you.
Ageless Hermes, farmers and merchants
        and thieves
pledge their faith to you;
        I pray to you as well.
Giver of fortune good and ill,
        grant me the good;
guardian of travellers,
        keep me safe on my journeys;
master of wit and charm,
        steady my stumbling tongue;
messenger of gods,
        give me sense to understand.

Aphrodite

I praise you, Aphrodite,
        goddess born of foam.
Fairest of all Olympos' maids,
        always precious
jewels adorn you, silks drape
        your unparalleled form.
With sweetly scented hair you come,
        your sea-green eyes
shine as stars, and all fall
        at your delicate feet.
You, who looks so kindly on lovers,
        I praise you.
You, who answers prayers of longing,
        I praise you.
You, whose gifts entrance all,
        young and old, I praise you.
You, who brings sweet bliss,
        who comforts the bereft,
who binds souls together,
        no heart can deny you.
Aphrodite, whose beauty
        would light the night sky,
I praise you and thank you
        for blessings given.

Glorious Aphrodite,
        my praise I offer you.
O mighty one,
        your irresistible power
overwhelms us mortals;
        helpless we obey you
and follow desire's demands
        despite all good sense.
Through you, O goddess,
        do we see with lovers' eyes
your own beauty
        reflected in our beloved.
Through you do new lovers
        welcome one another,
and old loves find their passion
        ever rekindled.
Aphrodite, whose gifts
        to humankind are great;
who nurtures growing love
        in the harshest of soils;
who so quickly impassions
        unsuspecting hearts;
Aphrodite—kind one, fierce one—
        I honor you.

Unsurpassed goddess,
        with love and awe I greet you.
Sea-green are your eyes,
        luminous and fathomless;
flawless is your form.
        O wondrous Aphrodite,
of water were you born,
        in water we know you—
in soft waves of pleasure,
        in torrents of desire,
in salt tears of lost love,
        in salt sweat at love's end.
So sweet your gifts, goddess,
        unbearably sweet,
so sharp their agony,
        so thin the line between.
For love that fills the soul;
        for life-giving passion;
for pure, clear, beautiful
        lust-maddened hearts;
for solace and hope;
        for love's comfort and terror:
O Aphrodite, for your blessings
        I thank you.

Aphrodite

Peerless Aphrodite,
        all beauty your gift,
all love your presence,
        all lovers wholly yours.
In kisses soft and savage,
        in jealous
agonies, in dreams
        of love forbidden,
in passions unwise,
        in torments of lust,
in these we feel your touch,
        exquisite goddess.
Aphrodite,
        bringer of unreason,
ruthless leveler
        of men and women,
giver of incomparable
        blessings,
we thank you for longing
        and fulfillment,
for soul-deep devotion,
        for flesh on flesh.
Aphrodite,
        we praise and honor you.

Gloried Aphrodite,
    goddess beyond all others,
wonders you bestow upon us,
    gifts so precious
and so dear,
    we thank you, awestruck,
    for your kindness.

Beautiful Aphrodite,
    child of the green sea,
you lift our souls, you bend our wills,
    you hold our hearts,
graceful one,
    we thank you, eager,
    for your blessings.

Beloved Aphrodite,
    piercing, shining light
of passion, heart's depth,
    inescapable goddess,
fair one,
    we thank you, blissful,
    for your favor.

Dear Aphrodite,
my heart is open to you,
you have blessed me with riches
uncounted, unknown.
Your gifts I prize,
your lessons I treasure,
heart-sinking hollowness,
joy fading in sunlight,
frivolous obsession,
pounding pulse kept secret;
sharp stab of ecstasy,
soft fog of completion;
vengeance given with precision,
taken eagerly;
small moments held close;
the illusion of control;
sudden slow tears in the night;
precious transcendence;
and always your presence,
like a cloak of fine silk,
a hand firm and subtle,
a delicate sureness.
Aphrodite, I offer my faith
and devotion.

Aphrodite, fairest
        of Olympos' jewels,
flawless in form, unsurpassed
        in grace and beauty.
Shining Aphrodite,
        constant your presence,
subtle your schemes,
        overwhelming your power,
irresistible your treasures.
        Kind-hearted one,
mistress of feeling,
        I praise and honor you.
O Aphrodite,
        who strips away self-control,
who leaves sweet desire in its place,
        I pray to you.
Glorious goddess, source of passion,
        I thank you
for precious moments of instinct,
        for fire and fury,
for the depth of pleasure,
        for the essence of need:
Aphrodite, dearest goddess,
        grant me your gifts.

A Prayer of Thanks to Aphrodite

Beloved Aphrodite,
dearest goddess, most worthy of praise,
I thank you for your blessings.
For love and for passion,
for loss and for longing,
for desire and for fulfillment,
for these I thank you,
for these I adore you,
for these I honor you.

A Prayer of Supplication to Aphrodite

Aphrodite, kind one, fair one,
companion in joy, comfort in despair,
if ever I have praised you,
if ever I have honored you,
if ever I have poured libations
or lauded you with hymns,
bless me now.

A Litany for Aphrodite

Aphrodite Aligena! Sea-Born Aphrodite,
who arose from foam upon the waves.
Aphrodite Aligena, we praise you! We honor you!

Aphrodite Kuprogenes! Aphrodite of Cyprus,
yours is that fair isle—Cyprian you are called.
Aphrodite Kuprogenes, we praise you! We honor you!

Aphrodite Pelagia! Aphrodite of the Sea,
whose soft embrace we feel in warm waters.
Aphrodite Pelagia, we praise you! We honor you!

Aphrodite Euplois! Aphrodite Fair-Sailing,
friend and guardian of sailors and seafarers.
Aphrodite Euplois, we praise you! We honor you!

Aphrodite Khruse! Golden Aphrodite,
fairer by far than all the treasures of the earth.
Aphrodite Khruse, we praise you! We honor you!

Aphrodite Pasiphaessa! Aphrodite the Far-Shining,
whose beauty would light the moonless night.
Aphrodite Pasiphaessa, we praise you! We honor you!

Aphrodite Philomeides! Laughter-Loving Aphrodite,
bringer of joy, mirth, and all sweet pleasures.
Aphrodite Philomeides, we praise you! We honor you!

Aphrodite Ambologera! Ever-Youthful Aphrodite,
always the most delightful of maids.
Aphrodite Ambologera, we praise you! We honor you!

Aphrodite Enoplios! Weapon-Bearing Aphrodite,
your fair form ready, resolute in defense.
Aphrodite Enoplios, we praise you! We honor you!

Aphrodite Summakhia! Aphrodite, Ally in War,
you lend your subtle strength and we are victorious.
Aphrodite Summakhia, we praise you! We honor you!

Aphrodite Areia! Aphrodite of Ares,
beloved of the war-god, you share his nature, hold his might.
Aphrodite Areia, we praise you! We honor you!

Aphrodite Androphonos! Aphrodite, Killer of Men,
fair you are and deadly can you be.
Aphrodite Androphonos, we praise you! We honor you!

Aphrodite Tumborukhos! Aphrodite Gravedigger,
you know of deaths both small and great.
Aphrodite Tumborukhos, we praise you! We honor you!

Aphrodite Skotia! Dark Aphrodite,
who leads us in love as quickly to the depths as to the heights.
Aphrodite Skotia, we praise you! We honor you!

Aphrodite Melainis! Black Aphrodite,
beneath the earth your dread power is known.
Aphrodite Melainis, we praise you! We honor you!

Aphrodite Morpho! Aphrodite of Many Shapes,
we know you as it pleases you to be known.
Aphrodite Morpho, we praise you! We honor you!

Aphrodite Hetaira! Aphrodite of Courtesans,
all loves and passions are within your realm.
Aphrodite Hetaira, we praise you! We honor you!

Aphrodite Genetullus! Aphrodite of Childbirth,
who women cry out to in joy and pain.
Aphrodite Genetullus, we praise you! We honor you!

Aphrodite Eleemon! Merciful Aphrodite,
with kindness you look upon us.
Aphrodite Eleemon, we praise you! We honor you!

Aphrodite Ourania! Heavenly Aphrodite,
as you were called of old, in distant lands.
Aphrodite Ourania, we praise you! We honor you!

Aphrodite Pandemos! Aphrodite of All People,
all of us who you bind together in love.
Aphrodite Ourania, we praise you! We honor you!

Ares

Great Ares I praise,
        bold one of the flashing eyes,
son of mighty Zeus
        and noble Hera you are,
beloved
        of golden sea-born Aphrodite.
You take joy in battle,
        the war-cry is your song.
Strength is yours, peerless warrior,
        and firm resolve,
and the pure, clear drive
        to defeat the enemy,
the battle rage that pushes us
        beyond our bounds
to achieve victory
        against a greater foe.
To the weak you lend strength;
        to the fearful, courage;
to those enslaved, the will
        to break the stoutest bonds.
Fierce Ares, you whose gifts
        ensure our survival,
O god of warriors,
        I praise and honor you.

Ares, unswerving ally
    of warriors,
swift is your sword-arm,
    steady your gaze.
In war-craft and instinct,
    in victory
at any cost, in strength
    from within,
in comradeship
    and in blind battle-rage,
in these we know your power,
    great war-god.
Ares, passionate one,
    the knowledge
of bodies is yours,
    familiar you are
with blood and pain,
    with the cost of success;
we thank you
    for needed savagery,
for understanding
    of the worth of life.
Solid Ares,
    we praise and honor you.

Ares, impetuous one
        who takes joy in strife,
keen-bladed god,
        beloved of Aphrodite.
Steadfast Ares, friend of those
        who struggle in vain,
giver of might drawn
        from desperation,
of skill born of muscle and bone,
        of devotion
to one's comrades, of proven worth,
        I honor you.
Bold Ares, fierce champion,
        unyielding foe,
you who survives, I pray to you.
        Peerless Ares,
in the single strike, the killing blow,
        we see you;
in strength of will,
        in battle joined in faith or fear,
in an unbroken spirit, we know you.
        Grant me strength,
son of Zeus, guide my hand at need,
        my heart at impact.

Hephaistos

Hephaistos

I praise you, Hephaistos,
    son of stately Hera,
for whom the flames dance
    as metal bends to your will.
You stand at the forge,
    bright sparks showering the dark
as would swiftly falling stars,
    while you work your art.
So great your skill, Hephaistos,
    such marvels you shape!
The most cunning devices
    have you created,
and exquisite jewelry
    to delight all eyes,
such that the gods themselves
    have never seen their like.
Invention is your gift,
    most able of craftsmen;
all those who create
    objects of need and beauty
feel your hands working through their own.
    Great Hephaistos,
patron of wrights, giver of skills,
    I honor you.

Hephaistos

Sturdy Hephaistos,
craftsman unequalled,
soul of fire and forge,
bringer of thought to fact.
In the lore
of intricate machines,
in precision and skill,
in calloused hands,
in nobility
within misfortune,
in these we see you,
mighty Hephaistos.
Hephaistos, strong-armed builder
of wonders,
creator
of delicate finery,
guide of artisans,
son of great Hera,
we thank you, Hephaistos,
for a keen eye,
for a deft hand,
for an artist's heart.
O Hephaistos,
we praise and honor you.

Noble Hephaistos,
unmatched armorer of gods,
master builder, strong-armed son
of Zeus and Hera.
Stout Hephaistos,
deliverer of Athena,
inventor of all manner
of clever device,
flawless forger of weapons
for gods and heroes,
firm-handed artisan,
I praise and honor you.
Hephaistos, patron of artist
and creator,
I pray to you. Well known were you
in times past;
many your temples,
joyous your festivals,
most needful god of skill and craft.
Guide my hands
in my work, grant me wit to devise
what is useful,
give me heart to create
what is beautiful.

Dionysos

Dionysos

To wild-haired Dionysos
I offer my praise,
son of Semele, who could not bear
the brilliance
of father Zeus
in all his pure magnificence,
beloved husband
to your dear Ariadne.
Wine and all its pleasures are yours,
Dionysos:
the intoxicating laughter
among great friends,
the uninhibited dance
of your devotees,
the soaring ecstasy
as you join in the dance,
the blessed oblivion,
the freedom from care,
the gift of transformation,
of insight, of change.
O Dionysos, bringer of joy
who reveals
all truths and secrets,
I praise you and honor you.

Dionysos

Sublime Dionysos,
 source of pleasure,
irresistible
 god of sensation.
In drops of sweet red wine
 on mortal tongues,
in rhythm so strong
 our hearts beat in time,
in bliss with no thought
 of consequence,
in these we feel you,
 son of Semele.
Dionysos, deep well
 of ecstasy,
swiftly-moving impulse
 and languid grace,
your gift the sheer plunge
 of transformation,
we thank you for knowledge
 gained in madness,
for seeing through wild eyes,
 for ripped-raw nerves.
Dionysos,
 we praise and honor you.

Dark-eyed Dionysos,
bringer of delight,
who gave sweet wine, its joys
and its perils, to man.
Dionysos, born of Zeus
and unknowing Semele—
Semele, burnt in the flames
of her lover's splendor,
a brief glimpse of the eternal,
paid for dearly—
fearful your wrath, overwhelming
your gifts, your power.
Dionysos, god who walks
in light and shadow,
I pray to you.
Grant me release from reason,
strength to step away from safety,
faith to follow
heart alone, will to close my eyes
to habit,
to follow impulse,
to let go of comfort,
to welcome change,
to bear what is torn away.

Pan

Pan

Glorious Pan I praise,
        dweller in the wilderness,
who roams through tangled woods,
        who walks the highest peaks
with step so light and sure.
        O Pan, goat-footed god,
splendid one, the lovely nymphs
        are your companions—
they follow you—they dance
        as you play your pipes.
Virility is your gift,
        and untamed passion,
O Pan; beasts and men alike
        receive your blessings.
Madness too can you give,
        sending us running
in fear and frenzy, blindly,
        no thought save escape.
Through you we see past
        civilization's sheer veil.
Through you we see revealed
        our nature and our strength.
O Pan, great Pan,
        I praise and honor you this day.

Pan

Joyful Pan, thoughtless
        and free of burden,
feeling, sense and instinct
        are your guides.
In thick-grown woods
        shadowed in sunshine,
in trickles of reasonless fear
        in our bones,
in ceaseless dance,
        in distant music,
in these we feel your presence,
        O great Pan.
Wondrous Pan,
        passionate son of Hermes,
uncivilized friend
        of beast and wild spirit,
you know the worth
        of a moment of life.
We thank you for long nights
        spent all in love,
for fear and frenzy,
        for desperate flight.
O mighty Pan,
        we praise and honor you.

Pan

Sure-footed Pan, overwhelming
force of abandon,
passion unbound and unfulfilled,
lightning-swift.
Great god of Arcadia,
dear son of Hermes,
mountain-dweller, friend
of the venturesome nymphs,
companion of Dionysos,
you play the pipes
sweetly, you leap and dance
with grace and daring.
Worthy Pan, god of the wild land
and the wild soul,
the sharp sheer edge of reason,
I pray to you.
Pan, who sends fear with no basis,
dread passing reason,
who seizes a soul
or a host swiftly, simply,
whose presence brings rapture,
whose touch inspires foresight,
O Pan, grant me your blessings,
spare me your terrors.

Eros

Eros

Eros, ancient one, swift impulse
        and raw power,
I praise you. Born of chaos,
        of love and conflict,
beautiful god, your arrows
        always hit their mark,
and when struck we are transformed.
        Bringer of passion;
of youthful innocence
        discovering first love;
of fiercely felt desire
        and of lust-driven need;
of love fulfilled;
        of a single bittersweet night
or a lifetime's rapture;
        of a love unreturned;
of blessed heights of ecstasy;
        of sweet despair,
of heart-sharp pain;
        of bliss passing understanding;
of purity of feeling;
        of clarity of heart—
Eros, capricious one,
        for these gifts I thank you.

Eros

Eros unbending,
strong-willed, unsubtle,
savage grace
and delicate awareness,
whispering in lovers' ears,
bringing us
your gift of ferocity.
Passion's god,
deftly you guide our hands,
our lips, our thoughts.
With fury and gratitude
we greet you;
we find pure joy
but never contentment,
more we seek, more you give,
more we become.
Eros unfathomable,
ancient one,
blinding, terrifying,
capricious,
inevitable.
Eros beautiful,
Eros unbearable,
beloved one,
compelling one.
Always I honor you!

Eros, whirlwind
    of sense and sensation,
blind irresponsible
    force behind life.
In flashes of raw need,
    in sudden lust,
in wretched souls
    praying for desire's end,
in savage pursuit
    of a single goal,
in these we know you,
    inevitable one.
Eros, revealer
    of harsh truths within,
guide of lovers true and false,
    pleasure's child,
swift storm of feeling,
    overwhelming urge,
we thank you
    for a step into passion,
for love taken, love given,
    love made.
Glorious Eros,
    we praise and honor you.

Eros

Eros, deep-hearted god, source of sweet need,
searing, purifying flame of desire,
agony we seek again and again,
unquestioned guide of those lost in feeling;

golden-winged god whose madness none may flee,
beautiful one whose will none may defy,
your gifts unbearable, ephemeral,
your blessings ceaseless, endless, limitless.

Great Eros, I pray to you, consume me,
bring me the essence of passion,
the wholeness of lust, the lightness of
completion. Bless me, Eros, with unreason.

Eros

Eros, lauded by all lovers,
knowing or no,
first and most constant companion
of Aphrodite.
Eros, source of all desire
and so of all life,
god of the senses,
of the body, of the heart,
you give us sweet need
and exquisite fulfillment
and take but our reason,
an exchange more than fair.
Unknowable Eros,
chief of the Erotes,
far-reaching one who none my escape,
I pray to you.
O Eros, whose gifts
enable our survival,
grant me a daring spirit,
a wide-open soul,
an ardent nature,
the will to follow passion.
Grant me the courage
of my own integrity.

Hekate

Hekate

Hekate I praise,
    fair maiden of the crossroad,
you who see things hidden,
    who heard Persephone
as she cried out
    from the underworld. Hekate,
with whose help did Demeter
    regain her dear child;
whose torches light the moonless night;
    who guards the gate;
who receives due offering
    wherever three roads meet;
yours, goddess, are shares
    in all the realms. Hekate,
who travels freely along all roads,
    I praise you.
To you, Hekate,
    are the mysteries known.
To you do women
    ever turn for protection.
To you do those who work magic
    pray for wisdom.
Hekate, ancient one,
    I praise and honor you.

Hekate

Hekate, wise one,
walker in the dark
who moves swiftly
along hidden pathways.
In bright flames in the night,
uncertain roads
made clear,
in shifting lucent visions,
in hard choices made,
in shadows embraced,
in all these
are you well known, Hekate.
Hekate,
knower of things unknown,
seer of things unseen,
guide of the lost,
guardian of spirits,
friend of the helpless,
we thank you for comfort
and for shelter,
for a despairing heart's flutter
of hope.
O Hekate,
we praise and honor you.

Hekate

Ever-watchful Hekate,
    fair one, ancient one,
fast friend of women,
    trusted guardian of the home.
Hekate, whose reach extends
    through all the worlds,
whose might and fearful wisdom
    are unsurpassed,
whose sharp ears alone
    heard the cries of Persephone,
who is honored above all others
    by great Zeus.
Gracious Hekate,
    who walks with sure step
on twisted paths and shadowed streets,
    I pray to you.
Grant me freedom from fear,
    calm born of certainty
and faith, protection from all ill,
    from all evil.
Hekate, kind one, keep safe
    my home and family,
shield my children from all harm,
    guard well my door.

A Prayer to Hekate

Hekate, sure-stepping maid, watcher at the gate,
honored by mighty Zeus above all others,
fair goddess who walks freely along all paths,
holder of shares in all the worlds. Hekate,
keeper of evil from the home, friend of women,
guardian of children, protector in fear and need.

Hekate, keen-eyed one of whom we know too little,
honored in ancient times at each home's door,
receiver of crossroad offerings, of mothers' prayers,
I ask of you, defend us now as you did then.
I call on you to guard my home, my family,
my children. Kind Hekate, I praise and honor you.

Glorious Hekate, well known by all in times past,
honored today as well in many guises,
on this dark night I pray to you, shining goddess.
Peerless Hekate, I pour out sweet wine to you,
I pray to you: safeguard my home, my household;
watch over my daughters; keep all ill from my door.

Persephone

Persephone

O Persephone,
fair daughter of Demeter,
I praise you. Maiden you were,
gathering flowers
with your dear companions;
swiftly were you taken
away by great Hades,
his bride and love to be,
and to rule by his side
in his dark, rich kingdom.
For a season do you dwell
in your husband's realm
—your mother's grief unbearable,
she mourns your loss,
the world turns cold, the verdant fields
grow dry and brown—
then return to your mother,
to the brilliant sun,
to the renewed bounty of the earth.
O goddess,
loveliest of all the jewels
of the underworld,
gentle queen of the dead,
I praise and honor you.

Persephone,
        crocus in the snow,
light and life
        of somber Hades' realm.
In the devotion
        of a mother and child,
in welcoming sorrow,
        in comforting grief,
in joy awakened,
        in sweet homecoming,
in these we know you,
        child of Demeter.
Persephone,
        queen of the underworld,
friend of those who mourn
        and those who are mourned,
bright jewel of the earth,
        fair flower of the field,
we thank you for hope,
        for patience, for faith,
for the longed-for return
        of great love.
Persephone,
        we praise and honor you.

Soft-stepping Persephone,
 sure-footed you go
through thick-grown fields and slick-stoned caves,
 each realm your own.
Fair-haired bride of Hades,
 bright Helios saw you taken,
torn from the world, from your mother's arms,
 to the deep
unknown, to the home of the dead,
 to reign as queen
over all who have passed
 from life, from family.
Persephone, child of the green earth,
 who knows well
of joy and of solemnity,
 I pray to you.
Garlanded with flowers,
 enthroned in darkness,
awesome in beauty,
 terrifying in might,
friend and guardian
 of those dear ones lost to us,
goddess who one day will rule us all,
 I praise you.

Asklepios

I praise Asklepios,
son of bright Apollo
and fair Koronis,
student of learned Cheiron,
greatest of healers
and first among physicians.
In dreams you come,
bringing healing to those in need.
Many great temples had you,
Asklepios,
in Epidaurus
and in all the provinces,
where the sick would come each day
to pray for your help;
where the suffering slept,
awaiting your wisdom;
where the healed left fine offerings
in gratitude.
No illness is beyond your power,
able one;
at your touch bones mend,
pain is soothed, and fevers cool.
Kindly Asklepios,
I praise and honor you.

Kind Asklepios,
        son of Apollo,
mender of many,
        patron of healers.
In gentleness of voice
        and skillful touch,
in hard-learned knowledge
        and in quick instinct,
in children returned
        to longed-for health.
In these we see you,
        great Asklepios.
Asklepios,
        maker of sound bodies,
honored in temples
        across the ancient world,
you cure all disease,
        you renew our lives.
We thank you
        for blessings given to all,
for we all will one day
        ask for your gift.
Asklepios,
        we praise and honor you.

Kind Asklepios, healer
whose touch brings relief
from sickness and pain,
able son of Apollo.
Asklepios, provider of health,
dearest of gifts;
destroyer of maladies
deadly and trifling;
rebuilder of bodies,
restorer of hope,
constant friend of humanity,
I honor you.
Asklepios, whose skill
passes all limits but one,
and that by will, not nature,
I pray to you.
Asklepios, you have kept
my family in good health,
you have answered my prayers
swiftly and surely.
Of your power and your mercy
I have no doubt;
in your favor and your good will
I have all faith.

Hail Asklepios, granter of good health,
doctor with no peer, you grant us relief
from pain and hurt, from sickness and plague.
Son of Koronis and bright Apollo,
father of compassionate Hygeia,
your touch brings us ease, your words, wisdom.
In sleep we seek your aid and advice,
in dreams we gain healing and direction.
Asklepios, patron of physicians,
we honor you with prayers and libations,
we honor you as well with our bodies,
with our efforts to keep fit and healthy.
O Asklepios, greatest of healers,
friend of mankind, we praise and honor you.

Tyche

Tyche

I praise you, Tyche,
        fair daughter of mighty Zeus,
whose splendid temples
        were found in every city.
Peerless one, those you favor
        receive all good things.
We do what we can in the world,
        noble goddess:
we do our work each day
        with diligence and care;
we plant our crops
        and tend to them devotedly;
we use the wisdom we possess
        to craft our lives.
And yet for all our efforts,
        some times we must fail,
some things we are given
        only by luck—by you!—
for your gift, goddess,
        is to bend the rules of chance.
O Tyche, to whom so many pray
        for good fortune,
benevolent goddess,
        I praise and honor you.

Tyche

Blessed Tyche,
guide of the unguided,
friend of the desperate,
light of the lost.
In risks taken
despite near-hopeless odds,
in impulses followed
to unknown ends,
in choices made lightly,
in foolish caprice,
in these we look for you,
beloved one.
Dear Tyche,
unpredictable goddess,
gentle giver
of undeserved fortune,
beautiful flickering flame
of chance,
we thank you
for sweet serendipity,
for pure dumb luck,
for the long shot made true.
Tyche, kind one,
we praise and honor you.

Nike

Nike

Nike I praise,
provider of victory;
bright companion you are
to glorious Athena,
patroness of soldiers,
of artists and athletes,
of all of us who join
in battle or contest,
who pray to you, O Nike,
for strength and fortune,
for your great gift of success.
Unsurpassed goddess,
we pray to you that our efforts
be rewarded,
that our foes not triumph
by trickery or guile,
that we may overcome all odds
and take the day.
Though we may lose a battle,
may we win the war,
may no defeat be final.
O shining Nike,
friend to all who strive,
I praise you and honor you.

Nike

Nike, able patroness
    of heroes,
clear-eyed granter
    of endurance and faith.
In crisp and precise plans
    of battle,
in swift, sudden changes
    of direction,
in effort rewarded,
    in goals achieved,
in these we feel your hand,
    honored Nike.
Nike, companion
    of great Athena,
fair one honored
    in distant Samothrace,
your chosen champions
    will ever prevail.
We thank you for help
    to the deserving,
for that last push
    toward well-earned victory.
Vibrant Nike,
    we praise and honor you.

Eileithuia

Eileithuia

Kind Eileithuia, helper of women,
friend of mothers, giver of easy births.
Honored by women long ago you were,
in fine temples. More ancient still your praise
in distant Amnisos, deep in a cave,
dark as the womb, pools of cool water within,
your image carved in stone, touched by prayerful hands
until it smoothed and shone. Daughter of Zeus
and noble Hera, many offerings
of sweet honey were you given of old,
still more will you be given in thanks.
Gentle Eileithuia, skillful goddess,
bring to me a quick labor and safe birth,
welcome with me a loved and healthy child.

Gaia

Blessed Gaia, mother of all,
I honor you.
All-encompassing one,
from chaos you arose;
you brought Ouranos into being,
O Gaia,
to father your children,
to make for them a home.
Mother you are
to many, titans and monsters;
grandmother you are
to Olympos' shining gods;
life-giver you are
to all who dwell on the earth.
O Gaia, kind one,
your gifts are without number—
the land on which we live,
the food we eat, the air—
all the world's wonders—
all of existence itself.
Revered goddess, for these things
and more we thank you.
Gaia, source of all life,
I praise and honor you.

Gaia

Bountiful Gaia,
mother of us all,
generations have passed
beneath your gaze.
In white-streaked skies,
in rock and mud and dirt,
in frigid blue waters
crowned with bright ice,
in heavy-fruited trees,
in birth, in death,
in these we see you,
beloved goddess.
Gaia, provider
of many treasures—
the blades of grass,
the mountains, the rivers,
the creatures of the wind,
the sea, the earth,
we thank you for all—
for fruit and grain,
for sweet water, for the air,
for our lives.
Blessed Gaia,
we praise and honor you.

To the Gods

A Devotion

Hestia, hearth-keeper, maidenly home-loving one,
dweller in the center, I praise and honor you.

Awesome Zeus, wielder of lightning, master of storms,
ruler of Olympos, I praise and honor you.

Hera of the lovely eyes, guardian of marriage,
graceful one, Zeus' fair bride, I praise and honor you.

Mighty Poseidon, at your will seas rise or calm.
Ocean-king, sailors' friend, I praise and honor you.

Demeter, good mother, you the seasons obey.
Honored harvest-bringer, I praise and honor you.

Great Hades, you who rules in the depths of the Earth,
wealth-holder, peace-bringer, I praise and honor you.

Grey-eyed Athena, weaver, wise one, warrior,
revered battle-maiden, I praise and honor you.

Far-shooting Apollo, seers' inspiration,
health-giver, brilliant one, I praise and honor you.

Agile Artemis, fair of form and fleet of foot,
huntress and markswoman, I praise and honor you.

Fierce Ares, strong and save, peerless warrior,
strength-giver, protector, I praise and honor you.

Aphrodite, glorious beauty, passion's mistress,
golden sea-born goddess, I praise and honor you.

Excellent Hephaistos, genius of fire and forge,
invention is your gift. I praise and honor you.

Swift-footed Hermes, guardian, guide and messenger,
light-hearted luck-bringer, I praise and honor you.

Wild-haired Dionysos, bringer of wine and dance,
music, joy and passion, I praise and honor you.

Gentle Persephone, Hades' young bride, mighty
queen who welcomes the dead, I praise and honor you.

Watchful Hekate, fair maiden of the crossroad,
you who see things hidden, I praise and honor you.

Skillful Asklepios, healer unparalleled,
all seek your gifts in time. I praise and honor you.

Goat-footed Pan of wild forests and mountain peaks,
sweetly you play the pipes. I praise and honor you.

Eros, ancient one, pure impulse and raw power,
swift-shooting heart-piercer, I praise and honor you.

Nike, to whom we pray for success in all things,
bringer of victory, I praise and honor you.

Tyche, luck-bringer, goddess of the saving throw,
yours is all good fortune. I praise and honor you.

Blessed Gaia, mother of all, giver of life,
all-encompassing one, I praise and honor you.

Blessed Hestia, center of the home, I praise you.
Awesome Zeus, ruler of Olympos, I praise you.
Great Hera, patroness of marriage, I praise you.
Poseidon, sea-king of awesome might, I praise you.
Revered Demeter, bountiful one, I praise you.
Hades, lord of wealth, lord of the dead, I praise you.
Wise Athena, warrior maiden, I praise you.
Bright Apollo, archer unerring, I praise you.
Artemis, mistress of animals, I praise you.
Clever Hermes, O swift-footed one, I praise you.
Golden Aphrodite, glorious one, I praise you.
Peerless Ares, ally of soldiers, I praise you.
Crafty Hephaistos, inventive one, I praise you.
Intoxicating Dionysos, I praise you.
Mighty Hekate, torch-bearing maiden, I praise you.
Fair Persephone, Hades' young queen, I praise you.
Artful Pan, roamer in wild places, I praise you.
Eros, swift impulse and raw power, I praise you.
Ancient Gaia, mother of us all, I praise you.
Asklepios, greatest of healers, I praise you.
Gracious Tyche, fortune is your gift. I praise you.
Honored Nike, granter of victory, I praise you.
And to all the gods and goddesses—I praise you!

To the Gods

Hestia, heart of the house, first born and last:
for light and warmth, home and hearth, we thank you.
One voice among many, I honor you.

Awesome Zeus, mightiest of all the gods:
protector and rain-bringer, we thank you.
One voice among many, I honor you.

Noble Hera, defender of marriage:
for family and fidelity, we thank you.
One voice among many, I honor you.

Poseidon, lord of the ocean depths:
friend to sailors and seafarers, we thank you.
One voice among many, I honor you.

Demeter, best of mothers, gracious one:
for fertile fields and fruit-filled trees, we thank you.
One voice among many, I honor you.

Hades, ruler of the vast underworld:
for a gentle end to a long life, we thank you.
One voice among many, I honor you.

Athena, grey-eyed daughter of great Zeus:
for wisdom, for skill, for victory—we thank you.
One voice among many, I honor you.

Shining Apollo, archer unerring:
for health, for art, for music—we thank you.
One voice among many, I honor you.

Artemis, first-born child of fair Leto:
protector of our children, we thank you.
One voice among many, I honor you.

Hermes, clever son of Zeus and Maia:
for wit and luck and humor, we thank you.
One voice among many, I honor you.

Glorious Aphrodite, kind one, fair one:
for love, for lust, for passion—we thank you.
One voice among many, I honor you.

Ares, who takes joy in combat and strife:
for strength, for will, for vigor—we thank you.
One voice among many, I honor you.

Skillful Hephaistos, maker of marvels:
for craft and invention, we thank you.
One voice among many, I honor you.

Dionysos, beautiful god of the vine:
for rapture and transcendence, we thank you.
One voice among many, I honor you.

Great Hekate, ever-watchful maiden:
torch-bearing guide and guardian, we thank you.
One voice among many, I honor you.

Persephone, lovely queen of the dead:
you who will welcome us all, we thank you.
One voice among many, I honor you.

Goat-footed Pan, roamer in wild places:
for instinct and unreason, we thank you.
One voice among many, I honor you.

Eros, irresistible force of desire:
for mindless, ruthless passion, we thank you.
One voice among many, I honor you.

Asklepios, wisest of physicians:
for health and for healing, we thank you.
One voice among many, I honor you.

Fair Tyche, provider of all good things:
for luck so kindly given, we thank you.
One voice among many, I honor you.

Nike, patron of athlete and soldier:
for all our victories, we thank you.
One voice among many, I honor you.

Gaia, ancient one on whose flesh we tread:
for our lives, for existence, we thank you.
One voice among many, I honor you.

About the Gods

Aphrodite

An ancient and powerful goddess with a pedigree linking her to Ishtar, Aphrodite is best known as a goddess of love, sex, and beauty.

Myth

There are several versions of the story of Aphrodite's birth; in the more interesting tale, when Kronos overthrew his father Ouranos by castrating him, his testicles fell into the sea, and Aphrodite was created from the foam, drifting until she landed on Cyprus. Thus Aphrodite is an older god even then Zeus and his siblings.

Another particularly famous story has her married to Hephaistos; in this story, when Hephaistos went off to work, her lover Ares came to her. When Hephaistos learned of this, he invented a cunning net to trap the lovers, making them immobile. Once they were trapped, he called all the gods to see them and make fun of them. Hermes, however, said that he would gladly be restrained as Ares was if only he could lie beside the beautiful Aphrodite! This story appears in the *Odyssey*; in the *Iliad*, Hephaistos has an entirely different spouse.

Aphrodite's affair with Anchises is also well known. In this story, she appears to Anchises, disguised as a mortal woman, offering to become his wife. Anchises wants to consummate the marriage immediately, and Aphrodite is agreeable. Afterward she reveals herself to him as a goddess, and he is terrified; she tells him that he must never tell who the true mother is of their child Aeneas.

Aphrodite is also known for aiding mortals in their love affairs, as in the story of Pygmalion and Galatea, in which the sculptor Pygmalion creates and falls in love with a beautiful statue; Aphrodite, taking pity on the smitten man, brings the statue to life and they presumably live happily ever after.

Worship

Aphrodite was honored throughout Greece, but her home was on the isle of Cyprus. She was honored during the following:

- *Aphrodisia,* a festival of Aphrodite Pandemos (of all people)
- *Arrephoria,* a small fertility ritual to Athena but also involving Aphrodite in the Gardens and Eros

In addition to her role as goddess of love, in some areas she was also known as a friend to sailors, her image taken to sea as a token of good luck.

She is honored on the fourth day of each month.

Apollo

Apollo is the son of Zeus and the twin brother of Artemis; his special interests are archery, music (particularly the lyre), and health and healing, as well as being god of plagues. His association with the sun came late to Greece.

Myth

Apollo's first story is of his birth, along with that of his twin Artemis; son of Zeus by Leto, his mother drew the wrath of Hera, who kept away the birth goddess Eileithuia so that Leto could not give birth. Finally the gods sent their messenger Iris, who let Eileithuia know that she was needed and promised her a golden necklace if she would come (possibly to induce her to risk Hera's anger); she did so, and Leto bore her children.

Another story of Apollo tells how he acquired the oracle at Delphi. There are several versions of this myth, but all tell how he killed the snake Python who had occupied the spot beforehand; in some stories Apollo is then punished for that act.

Apollo is also known for a series of unfortunate love affairs with nymphs and mortal women, many of whom were far from eager to have a god for a lover; for example, he pursued the nymph Daphne, but she so feared him that she prayed to Zeus, who turned her into a laurel tree.

Worship

Apollo, while honored throughout Greece, had particularly strong centers of worship in Delos (his birthplace) and Delphi (the site of his oracle). He was celebrated in a number of festivals, including the following:

- *Thargelia,* a festival in which Apollo received first-fruits offerings; this festival also featured a purification ritual involving Pharmakoi, human scapegoats who were run out of town, symbolically taking all the ills of the city with them
- *Pyanepsia,* a fertility ritual including the Eirisione, an olive branch wrapped in wool and decorated with various objects, which bands of boys brought to the houses of the city in exchange for gifts, the bough bringing good fortune and fertility to the house

He was also honored on the seventh day of each month.

Ares

Ares is god of war, particularly of its instinctive, survive-at-all-costs aspects.

Myth

Despite being a war god, Ares' stories of battle are often less than complimentary. When he and Athena are at odds (as in the Iliad), she always gets the better of him. She seems to be more of a strategist, while Ares is a god of the common soldier or warrior.

In fact, Ares in general seems to receive little or no respect; he is easily the least favored child of Zeus and Hera.

He is also known as Aphrodite's lover. When Hephaistos (in one source the husband of Aphrodite) went off to work, her lover Ares came to her. Ares and Aphrodite are said to have had three children, Phobos, Deimos, and Harmonia.

Worship

I do not know of any festivals to Ares; although he was offered to by soldiers in battle, his temples were rare and he does not seem to have been commonly worshipped outside of combat situations.

Artemis

Artemis, sister of Apollo and also an archer, is known as a goddess of the hunt as well as of animals and wildlife. Her companions are the nymphs, with whom she dances and roams the wilderness. She is also a goddess who can assist in childbirth, and a protector of young children. Her association with the moon came late to Greece.

Myth

Artemis shares her first story with her twin Apollo, her birth; in some versions of this tale, she is born first and even helps with her brother's delivery.

In myth Artemis is not particularly friendly to mortals; in fact she can be deadly, and several of her myths have to do with her killing mortals who have somehow offended her. Along with her brother Apollo, she killed all of Niobe's children when Niobe dared to compare her large brood to Leto's two. She is also known to have slain several of her companions after they were seduced by Zeus.

Artemis is one of the three virgin goddesses, along with Hestia and Athena; Aphrodite has no power over her.

Worship

Artemis was one of the most widely-worshipped and most ancient Hellenic deities. She was celebrated in a number of festivals, including the following:

- *Elaphebolia,* a festival of Artemis Elaphebolios (deer hunter), when a stag was sacrificed to the goddess; when stags became too rare, pastry substitutes replaced this offering
- *Charisteria,* a festival of thanksgiving to Artemis Agrotera (goddess of the hunt) and Enyalios (Ares)
- *Mounichia,* when Artemis was offered small cakes similar to those offered to Hekate at crossroads.

She was also honored on the sixth day of each Greek month.

Asklepios

Asklepios, son of Apollo, is god of healing and medicine. Born mortal, he died, but somehow eventually attained a unique status between god and hero.

Myth

Asklepios, taught by the centaur Cheiron to be a great healer, crossed a line when he attempted to raise the dead, and Zeus struck him down with a thunderbolt. In anger, Apollo kills the Cyclops who created the thunderbolt in the first place, and was made to serve a mortal for a year in punishment. (This death, however, seems to have had little effect on Asklepios' popularity.)

Worship

A widely popular god, Asklepios' worship spread rapidly, and his healing sanctuaries arose throughout Greece as soon as he was introduced. Those in need of healing visited these sanctuaries, hoping for healing, or for a dream telling them of a cure for their malady.

Athena

As patron goddess of Athens, Athena was a very popular deity with many myths attributed to her and a number of festivals in her honor. Her areas of interest were quite diverse—she was a goddess of war, of wisdom, and of weaving and other crafts.

Myth

Athena's first story is that of her birth. Her father Zeus had received a prophecy that a child born by him of Metis (wisdom) would overthrow him, as he had overthrown his father Kronos and as Kronos had overthrown his father Ouranos. To solve this small problem, he swallowed the pregnant Metis. However, some time later Zeus was afflicted with a prodigious headache, so agonizing that he asked Hephaistos to strike him on the head with an axe. Hephaistos did so, and Athena leaped out, fully grown and fully armored.

Athena is well known for her patronage of heroes, such as Odysseus, who she aids in his long journey home from the Trojan War.

However friendly to mortals Athena may have been in general, she was also as capable of any of the gods of striking in anger, as shown in the story of Arachne, who challenged the goddess to a weaving contest and was subsequently transformed into a spider. As one of the three virgin goddesses (along with Artemis and Hestia), Athena never married or took a lover, but she was once pursued by Hephaistos, and later took an interest in his child Erichthonios.

Worship

Above all Athena was the patron goddess of the city of Athens, but she was honored throughout Greece. She was celebrated in a great number of festivals, including the following:

- *Arrephoria,* a small fertility ritual also involving Aphrodite and Eros
- *Khalkeia,* a festival of craftsmen (especially bronze-workers) for Athena and Hephaistos, during which women began weaving a peplos to be later offered to Athena
- *Kallynteria,* a festival during which Athena's temple was cleaned
- *Panathenaia,* probably Athena's largest festival, involving the presentation to the goddess of the peplos begun during the Khalkeia; in later years athletic contests were also held at this time
- *Plynteria,* a festival during which a cult image (statue) of Athena was annu ally washed

She was honored as well on the third day of each Greek month.

Demeter

Demeter was known as a goddess of grain—of fertility, of successful harvests—and therefore a very important deity for an agrarian people. As the devoted mother of Persephone, she is the most maternal of any of the Greek goddesses.

Myth

Demeter's best known myth is of course the story of the abduction of her daughter, Persephone, by Hades. In her anguish she caused the earth to become barren, and would not renew its fertility until Persephone was returned; however, while in the underworld Persephone had eaten several pomegranate seeds—and, having eaten in the underworld, she had to stay there for some months of the year. Each year, while Persephone was with her mother, the earth was fruitful; but when she went to be with her husband, Demeter's mourning caused the infertile season of the year.

Another story of Demeter has to do with Poseidon's pursuit of her, and her self-transformation into a horse in an attempt to avoid his advances (not a good plan given Poseidon's own connection with horses—he turned into a stallion and succeeded in gaining his desire).

Yet another tale tells how Demeter punished Erysichthon for cutting down the trees in one of her sacred groves, and for threatening her with an axe when, in disguise, she attempted to stop him. It was a particularly nasty punishment: she gave him an insatiable hunger that caused him to eat everything in his home, to become a beggar, and finally—when there was nothing left—to devour himself.

Worship

Demeter's worship was widespread; she was honored in numerous festivals, including:

- The Eleusian Mysteries, easily the most important of Demeter's festivals, drew men and women from all over Greece. The rituals were secret, and the participants kept these secrets so well that we know almost nothing about them; however, they seem to have had something to do with guaranteeing initiates a better place in the afterlife.
- *Haloa,* a festival to Demeter and Dionysos involving explicit sexual language and imagery, very likely a fertility festival
- *Skira,* a women's fertility festival
- *Stenia,* a women's festival preceding the Thesmophoria, of which little is known.
- *Thesmophoria,* a women's festival of which, again, little is known, although it seems to have been connected with fertility

Dionysos

Dionysos is god of wine, theater, and ecstasy. He was particularly loved and worshipped by women.

Myth

The story of Dionysos' birth is a dramatic one. His mother, Semele, was a lover of Zeus. Hera discovered the affair, and went in disguise to Semele, urging her to ask Zeus to show himself to her in his true form. Semele did so, but was unable to bear the sight of Zeus in all his godly glory. Semele died, but Zeus rescued the child she was carrying, keeping it safe in his thigh until it was time for him to be born.

He is also well known for his love for and marriage to Ariadne, a mortal woman who he had made immortal, who had been first seduced and abandoned by Theseus (or perhaps she was taken by Dionysos, there are confilcting versions of this story).

Dionysos was as inclined as any of the gods to seek vengeance for slights. In one story, he is captured by pirates, bound, and taken to sea. His bonds fall off, convincing only the helmsman that he is in fact a god; the other pirates scoff until vines grow through the ship. Dionysos transforms into a lion, and all but the helmsman leap into the sea, turning into dolphins.

Worship

While most of Greek religious practice supported the community, Dionysian ritual often focused more on the individual, with a greater emphasis on mysticism and transcendent experience. A god very different from the rest of the pantheon, Dionysos was celebrated in a number of festivals, including the following:

- *Anthesteria,* a three-day wine-drinking festival. On the first day the jars were opened and the new wine tasted; on the second day, more wine was drunk, and the symbolic marriage between Dionysos and the wife of the Basileus (an official in charge of various religious festivals) occurred; on the third day, offerings were made to Hermes on behalf of the dead
- City *Dionysia,* a festival very much like the Country *Dionysia* but featuring theatrical tragedies
- Country *Dionysia,* a festival involving a phallic procession, theatrical comedies, and contests
- *Oschophoria,* a festival to Dionysos held on the same day as Apollo's *Pyanepsia*

Eileithuia

Eileithuia is a goddess of childbirth; nothing is known of her beyond that single function.

Eros

Eros is a god of love and passion. His depiction as a young boy with wings and a quiver is relatively late.

Myth

Several different origins are given for Eros. In one, he is simply (simply!) the son of Aphrodite; in others he is given various pedigrees. More interesting, however, is the version in which first there was only Chaos, from which first Gaia, then Tartaros, and finally Eros emerged, making him one of the oldest deities, and certainly a force to be reckoned with.

Gaia

Gaia, mother Earth, is an ancient deity not commonly the recipient of prayer by the ancients; however, she is certainly worthy of any and all honor.

Myth

Gaia emerged from Chaos and created Ouranos, to be her mate and bear her children; among these children were the Titans, including Kronos and Rhea, who bore Zeus and his siblings. Gaia, the earth, is the mother of all.

Hades

Hades is lord of the dead, ruler of the underworld to whom all the earth's subterranean treasures belong.

Myth

Hades is best known for his marriage to Persephone. With the permission of her father Zeus (but with neither the permission nor the knowledge of her mother Demeter), he took her away to his kingdom under the earth. Demeter, in mourning for her lost daughter, made the earth barren until her daughter was returned; however, since Persephone had eaten several pomegranate seeds while in Hades' realm, from then on she spent part of each year with Hades and part with her mother.

Hades also appears in the story of the apportioning of the earth between his brothers and himself. Zeus received the earth, Poseidon the sea, and Hades the underworld–which displeased him until he learned that he would also receive all precious gems and metals under the earth, making him a god of wealth as well.

Many of Hades' other appearances in myth have to do with rare living mortals such as Orpheus visiting his realm.

Hekate

Hekate, goddess of pathways and crossroads, is also associated with magic. She is often accompanied by dogs. She was never, in antiquity, depicted as a crone or old woman.

Myth

Not a lot is known of Hekate; however, she is said to have received a share of earth, sea and sky, and is well-respected by Zeus.

When Demeter's daughter Persephone was abducted, it was Hekate who heard her cries and told Demeter what had happened.

Worship

Hekate received offerings at crossroads; she may have originated in Caria, and her most important center of worship was Lagina. She was especially dear to women. Many homes had a *hekataion*—a small shrine to Hekate—at the door.

Hephaistos

Hephaistos is god of smiths, craftsmen and inventors, particularly metal-workers.

Myth

Hephaistos' first myth is that of his birth to Hera; he may or may not be the son of Zeus as well (if he is not, he is then Hera's alone). In any case, he was born lame, and Hera rejected him, throwing him out of Olympos to the earth, where he was raised by Thetis.

Another story tells of Hephaistos' revenge against Hera. He makes for her a beautiful throne and presents it to her. Pleased with the gift, she sits in it—and is immediately stuck. Eventually, of course, Hephaistos frees his mother from this trap, having been convinced to do so by Dionysos following a bout of drinking.

He also takes part in the story of Athena's birth, acting as the "midwife" who frees her from Zeus' head by a blow with an axe.

In one of Hephaistos' tales, he is married to Aphrodite. This story appears only in the Odyssey; in the Iliad, Hephaistos has an entirely different spouse, Charis.

Worship

Although in many parts of Greece Hephaistos was less important than some other gods, in Athens Hephaistos was well honored (due at least in part to his fatherhood of Athens' first king, Erichthonios) and is celebrated at several festivals, including the following:

- *Hephaesteia,* of which little is known, not even the date; it is known to have included a torch race
- *Khalkeia,* a festival of craftsmen (especially bronze-workers) for Athena and Hephaistos.

Hera

Hera, wife of Zeus and queen of the gods, is one of those deities whose mythology does not quite reflect her worship. She is primarily known as a goddess of marriage, specifically of the legal/contractual aspects of marriage, and is especially to be called on at weddings.

Myth

Most of Hera's myths, unfortunately, have to do with her jealousy and her poor treatment of Zeus' other women, such as Semele, or of his children by these women, such as Herakles. As a goddess of marriage, this certainly makes some sense.

She is also known for her difficult relationship with her son Hephaistos, who may or may not have been fathered by Zeus (if not, he was the child of Hera alone). According to one myth, when she gave birth to him and discovered that he was imperfect—lame—she threw him out of Olympos immediately.

Worship

Hera was widely worshipped all over Greece, particularly in Argos and in Samos. The greatest, earliest known temples were hers. She was honored in various festivals, including:

- *Gamelia,* a festival honoring the sacred marriage of Zeus and Hera
- The Great *Daedela,* held every sixty years in Boetia, in which an altar and wooden statues are constructed, used, and entirely burned
- *Heraia,* a New Year festival celebrated in Argos

In the deme of Erchia, she was honored as Hera Thelchinia (Goddess of Charm)

Hermes

Hermes is the god of tradesmen and travellers, as well as thieves. As a god of communication he helps with the transmission of messages. He also acts as a psychopomp—one who conducts the dead to their new residence—as well as a more general messenger and escort.

Myth

Hermes' first myth has to do with his birth and first day of life; his first action was to take a tortoise and make a lyre from its shell. Later that day, he went to find his brother Apollo's herds of cows, which he stole, driving them backwards in order to trick Apollo into searching in the wrong direction. When Apollo confronted him, he denied everything—after all, he was only a baby newly born! Apollo brought the young Hermes to Olympos, where he apologized and gave Apollo his newly created lyre, and all was well.

He also appears in many myths in his role as escort or psychopomp; perhaps the best known of these tales is when he brings Persephone back to her mother.

Worship

Although Hermes had no major festivals of his own, he was quite popular in the countryside, especially in Arcadia. People would create piles of stones, known as herms, in his honor (in later times more artistic herms would be made).

He was also honored on the fourth day of each month.

Hestia

Hestia, goddess of the hearth, is the least anthropomorphized of any of the major deities of her pantheon, despite her central place in Greek religion. Her interest is primarily in the home.

Myth

Hestia has very little mythology in comparison with her sibling gods. One of the Olympians, she was first born of Rhea and first swallowed by her father Kronos; she was also last to be reborn when Zeus caused Kronos to disgorge all of his brothers and sisters.

It is also well known that Hestia is one of three virgin goddesses (along with Artemis and Athena) who are immune to Aphrodite's powers. Although eagerly sought after by Poseidon and Apollo, she asked Zeus if she might remain a virgin and occupy the hearth of the home, and this he granted.

Worship

Hestia's worship took place primarily in the home rather than in public ritual. Her name, in Greek, means "hearth," and in many ways she is identified with that center of every home. Libations were made at the hearth, as were the small offerings of food made to her at each meal or family sacrifice.

Nike

Goddess of victory, Nike is closely associated with Athena. The well known statue of the Winged Victory of Samothrace represents her. She did not have a wide-spread cult following.

Pan

Pan is a rustic god of shepherds and wild places; he is also known to cause "panic"—a sudden irrational terror. He was not, as has sometimes been assumed from his name, any sort of universal deity.

Myth

Pan, the child of Hermes and the daughter of Dryops, was born with the horns and feet of a goat. Hermes was delighted, and brought his new son to Olympos to show him off, where all the gods thought he was splendid.

Pan was known for his love affairs, which sometimes ended badly, as with his passion for Echo, who fled him until she became, well, an echo.

Worship

Originally a god of Arcadian shepherds, Pan's worship later spread through Greece, where he was often honored along with the nymphs, in caves and grottos.

Persephone

Persephone is known primarily for her relationships with other gods—as the daughter of Demeter, and as the wife of Hades. She therefore can be associated with the spring, and with the turning of the seasons, as well as being one to pray to on behalf of the dead.

Myth

Persephone's myth is the story of her abduction by Hades. In Demeter's anguish she caused the earth to become barren, and would not return its fertility until Persephone was returned; however, while in the underworld Persephone had eaten several pomegranate seeds—and, having eaten in the underworld, she had to stay there for some months of the year. Each year, while Persephone was with her mother, the earth was fruitful; but when she went to be with her husband, Demeter's mourning caused the infertile season of the year.

Worship

Persephone, along with her mother Demeter, was celebrated in a number of festivals, including the following:

- The Eleusian Mysteries, easily the most important of Demeter's festivals, was as much a festival of Persephone and drew men and women from all over Greece. The rituals were secret, and the participants kept these secrets so well that we know almost nothing about them; however, they seem to have had something to do with guaranteeing initiates a better place in the afterlife.
- *Thesmophoria,* a women's fertility festival of which little is known

Poseidon

Best known as the god of the sea and a patron of sailors, Poseidon is also god of earthquakes, as well as of horses.

Myth

Poseidon has relatively few myths apart from his actions in the Iliad, and many of those have to do with his various mates and children. (He is said to be married to the nereid Amphitrite; fortunately for Poseidon, she does not appear to share Hera's jealous nature, and Poseidon has an easier time of it in this respect than his brother Zeus.) Another story of Poseidon has to do with the apportioning of the world between his brothers, Zeus and Hades, and himself: Zeus took the earth, Hades the underworld, including all its treasures, and Poseidon of course received the sea.

Worship

A very old god, Poseidon's good will was important to the seafaring Greeks. Poseidon was honored on the eighth day of each month.

It seems likely that a festival for Poseidon took place during the Greek month of Poseideon, but there is no record of it.

Tyche

Tyche, goddess of good fortune and "the saving throw," is especially honored by gamblers and others whose fate has fallen from their hands.

Myth

A divinity considered allegorical by many, Tyche has no mythology apart from a pedigree.

Worship

Tyche rose to popularity in the sixth century BCE; in later times she gained a greater importance, and was even named the city goddess in some areas.

Zeus

Zeus, first and strongest among the Olympians, may be best known for casting the thunderbolt, causing thunder and lightning and bringing storms to the earth. However, he is also very much concerned with issues of law and justice (oaths were made by his name), and is also (as Zeus Meilichios) a protective deity associated with the home and family.

Myth

Zeus' first story is a crucial one, one which works to establish the structure of the world as we know it. His father, Kronos, feared that one of his children would one day take over his position as "head god"; therefore, whenever his wife Rhea gave birth, Kronos would immediately swallow the infant, thereby preserving his own power. Rhea, of course, soon tired of this arrangement and eventually managed to save the youngest child—Zeus—by giving Kronos a rock wrapped in swaddling clothes instead, and sending Zeus into hiding. When Zeus reached manhood, he forced his father, by means of an emetic, to disgorge all of his siblings—Hestia, Poseidon, Demeter, Hades, and his bride-to-be Hera—and fulfilled Kronos' worst fears.

Some of the best-known myths of Zeus have to do with his many love affairs with nymphs and mortal women, affairs which often ended badly for the woman when Hera sought revenge against her: Leda, who he wooed as a swan, and who bore him Helen (eventually to be Helen of Troy), and the twins Kastor and Polydeukes (Castor and Pollux); Europa, who he abducted in the form of a bull; Io, who he seduces and then changes into a cow when caught by Hera; and Semele, mother of Dionysos who was destroyed when Hera tricked her into asking Zeus to show himself to her in his true, unbearable form. Many of these dalliances resulted in the birth of heroes and other notable men and women, although certainly Hera would not have felt that the ends justified the means.

Worship

Zeus was worshipped all over Greece, belonging equally to all. He is celebrated in a number of festivals, including the following:

- *Diasia,* a festival honoring and propitiating Zeus Meilichios with bloodless sacrifices
- *Dipolieia,* an ancient and unusual festival in which, following the sacrifice of an ox, the ax used in the ceremony is brought to trial and thrown into the sea
- *Olympieia,* a festival for Zeus Olympios, featuring sports competitions, particularly those having to do with horses.
- *Pompaia,* another festival to Zeus Meilichios, focusing on the survivial of the crops
- *Gamelia,* a festival honoring the sacred marriage of Zeus and Hera

He was also honored in the home as Zeus Ktesios and Zeus Meilichios, as protector of the home and the larder.

References

Burkert, Walter. *Greek Religion.* Harvard University Press, Cambridge, 1985.

Gantz, Timothy. *Early Greek Myth, Volumes 1 and 2.* Johns Hopkins University Press, Baltimore, 1993.

Kerenyi, Karl. *The Gods of the Greeks.* Thames and Hudson, London, 1951.

Johnston, Sarah Iles. *Restless Dead: Encounters between the Living and the Dead in Ancient Greece.* University of California Press, Berkeley, 1999.

Nilsson, Martin P. *Greek Folk Religion.* University of Pennsylvania Press, Philadelphia, 1940.

Parke, H.W. *Festivals of the Athenians.* Thames and Hudson, London, 1977.

Simon, Erika. *Festivals of Attica: An Archaeological Commentary.* University of Wisconsin Press, Madison, Wisconsin, 1983.

www.ingramcontent.com/pod-product-compliance
Ingram Content Group UK Ltd.
Pitfield, Milton Keynes, MK11 3LW, UK
UKHW040601210726
13854UKWH00008B/1711